BEARPORT BIOGRAPHIES

MICHELLE OBAMA

ADVOCATE AND ROLE MODEL

by Rachel Rose

Consultant: Angela High-Pippert, Professor of Political Science,
University of St. Thomas
St. Paul, Minnesota

Minneapolis, Minnesota

Credits

Cover and title page, © BET Awards 2020/Getty Images; 4, © Michael Donhauser/picture alliance/Getty Images; 5, © Nima Taradji/Polaris/Newscom; 6, © Daniel Acker/Bloomberg/Getty Images; 7, © Andy Wong/UPI/Newscom; 8, © Jay Yuan/Shutterstock; 10, © Matt McClain/The Washington Post/Getty Images; 11, © FeyginFoto/Shutterstock; 12, © Ralf-Finn Hestoft/Corbis/Getty Images; 13, © Olivier Douliery/Abaca Press/Tribune News Service/Getty Images; 14, © Kent Nishimura-Pool/Getty Images; 15, © Pete Souza; The White House; 16, © Amanda Lucidon; The White House; 17, © Mark Wilson/Getty Images; 18, © Ralf-Finn Hestoft/Corbis/Getty Images; 19, © Tech. Sgt. James Hodgman/U.S. Air Force; 20, © Kevin Dietsch-Pool/Getty Images; 21, © Bennett Raglin/ESSENCE/Getty Images; 22R, © Matt McClain/The Washington Post/Getty Images; 22L, © Jay Yuan/Shutterstock

President: Jen Jenson
Director of Product Development: Spencer Brinker
Editor: Allison Juda
Photo Research: Book Buddy Media

Library of Congress Cataloging-in-Publication Data

Names: Rose, Rachel, 1968- author.
Title: Michelle Obama : advocate and role model / by Rachel Rose.
Description: Minneapolis, Minnesota : Bearport Publishing Company, [2021] | Series: Bearport biographies | Includes bibliographical references and index.
Identifiers: LCCN 2020039247 (print) | LCCN 2020039248 (ebook) | ISBN 9781647477196 (library binding) | ISBN 9781647477271 (paperback) | ISBN 9781647477356 (ebook)
Subjects: LCSH: Obama, Michelle, 1964- | Presidents' spouses--United States--Biography. | African American lawyers--Biography. | Political activists--Biography.
Classification: LCC E909.O24 R67 2021 (print) | LCC E909.O24 (ebook) | DDC 973.932092 [B]--dc23
LC record available at https://lccn.loc.gov/2020039247
LC ebook record available at https://lccn.loc.gov/2020039248

Copyright © 2021 Bearport Publishing Company. All rights reserved. No part of this publication may be reproduced in whole or in part, stored in any retrieval system, or transmitted in any form or by any means, electronic, mechanical, photocopying, recording, or otherwise, without written permission from the publisher.

For more information, write to Bearport Publishing, 5357 Penn Avenue South, Minneapolis, MN 55419. Printed in the United States of America.

Contents

Writing Rock Star 4
Humble Beginnings 6
Working Life 10
First Mom, First Lady 14
A New Chapter 20

Timeline 22
Glossary 23
Index 24
Read More 24
Learn More Online 24
About the Author 24

Writing Rock Star

Michelle Obama stepped onto the stage of the sold-out **stadium** in Chicago. The crowd of 14,000 fans roared and clapped for their hometown hero. They were excited to hear Michelle talk with Oprah Winfrey about her new book, *Becoming*. The former First Lady was hitting the road to tell the story of her life on a huge book tour.

Michelle's book

Every event of Michelle's book tour quickly sold out, including those in cities across Europe and Canada.

Oprah *(left)* and Michelle *(right)* spoke at the first stop on Michelle's book tour.

Humble Beginnings

Michelle LaVaughn Robinson was born on January 17, 1964, in Chicago, Illinois. Her family lived in a **working-class** neighborhood on Chicago's South Side. Although her family didn't have much, Michelle was raised by loving parents who believed education was very important. They taught Michelle and her older brother, Craig, to read by the time they were four years old.

Michelle's family lived on the top floor of this home in Chicago.

Michelle and Craig slept in the living room of their small home. Their beds were separated by a hanging sheet.

Michelle's mother, Marian Robinson *(left)*, lived in the White House and often traveled with Michelle and her family during their time as the First Family.

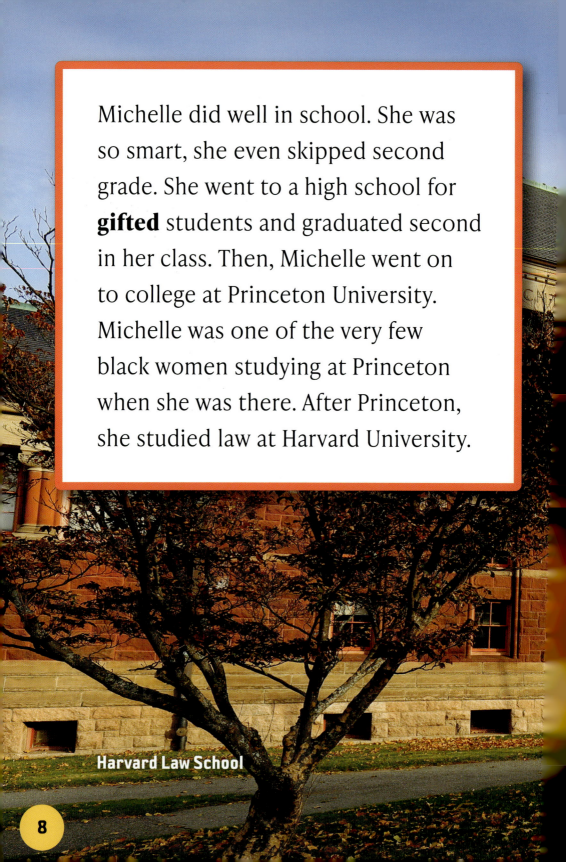

Michelle did well in school. She was so smart, she even skipped second grade. She went to a high school for **gifted** students and graduated second in her class. Then, Michelle went on to college at Princeton University. Michelle was one of the very few black women studying at Princeton when she was there. After Princeton, she studied law at Harvard University.

Harvard Law School

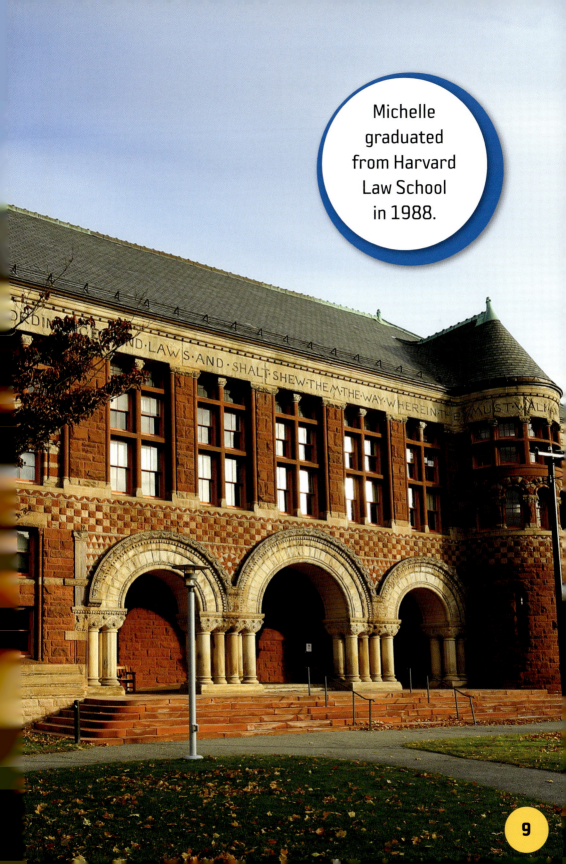

Michelle graduated from Harvard Law School in 1988.

Working Life

After law school, Michelle got her first job at a law firm in Chicago. But she soon realized she didn't like being a lawyer. She wanted to work in the community so she could help improve peoples' lives. In 1991, she left her job and went to work as an assistant to Chicago's mayor.

Michelle and Barack

In 1989, Michelle met her future husband, Barack Obama, at the law firm where she worked. She was Barack's **mentor**.

Michelle worked at Chicago City Hall

Michelle married Barack in 1992. She continued to build her new **career** as Barack started his work in **politics**. Michelle worked in jobs that helped students and other young people in the community. By the time Barack was running for president, Michelle had a top job at the University of Chicago Medical Center.

Michelle Obama is a powerful speaker.

In 2008, Michelle left her job so she could help Barack run for president. She made many speeches for his **campaign**.

Michelle supported Barack during his campaign.

First Mom, First Lady

When Barack became president in 2009, Michelle's top **priority** was their two daughters, Malia and Sasha. She wanted them to have as normal of a childhood as possible. She made sure they had family dinners together. And even though the White House had plenty of people who would cook and clean for them, Michelle gave her daughters **chores** to do.

The Obamas often traveled to Hawaii, where Barack was born.

Malia was 10 and Sasha was 7 when they moved into the White House.

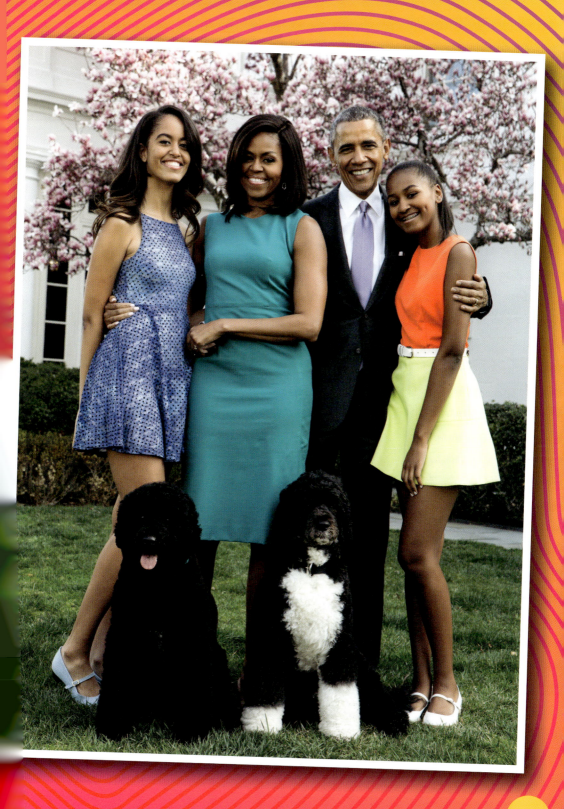

When she wasn't making sure her girls were growing up right, Michelle Obama was busy in her role as First Lady. In 2010, she started a program called *Let's Move!* The goal was to end childhood **obesity**. It encouraged kids to exercise and to eat a healthy diet. Michelle grew a vegetable garden at the White House as part of the project.

Michelle invited a group of Girl Scouts to a campout at the White House as part of *Let's Move! Outside*.

Children from the area came and helped at the White House vegetable garden.

Another project close to Michelle's heart was helping military families. She worked hard to support U.S. troops returning home from other countries. She made a program that provided education and training so that **veterans** could get jobs when they were done with their time in the military.

Education has always been important to Michelle. Her *Let Girls Learn* program helped more girls around the world go to school.

The program Michelle started for the military was called *Joining Forces*.

A New Chapter

Michelle and her family left the White House in 2017. After that, she started an exciting new chapter in her life. She continued to be an **advocate** for youth, particularly girls. In 2018, she became a best-selling author with her book *Becoming*. Michelle hopes that her book will inspire people to follow their dreams.

Michelle and Barack leaving the White House for the last time

Michelle launched the Michelle Obama Podcast in July 2020.

Michelle continues to speak up for what she believes in.

Timeline

Here are some key dates in Michelle Obama's life.

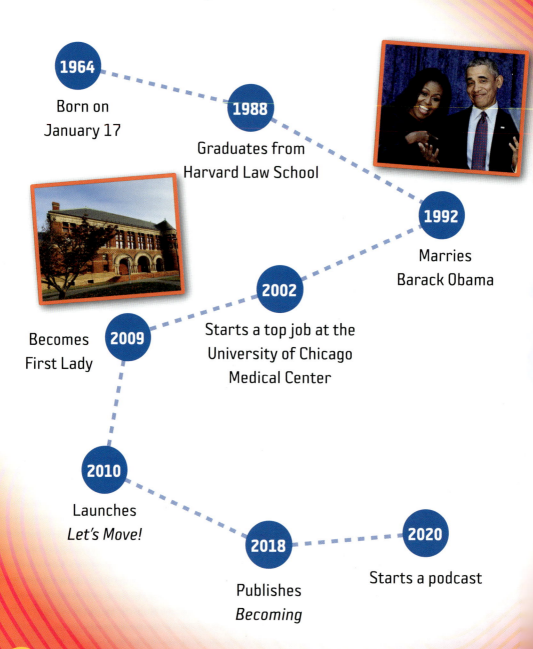

1964 Born on January 17

1988 Graduates from Harvard Law School

1992 Marries Barack Obama

2002 Starts a top job at the University of Chicago Medical Center

2009 Becomes First Lady

2010 Launches *Let's Move!*

2018 Publishes *Becoming*

2020 Starts a podcast

Glossary

advocate someone who supports a cause that is important to them

campaign an attempt to win a political office

career the job a person has for a long period of time

chores small jobs that are done regularly around the home

gifted having a special talent for something

mentor a person who guides or helps people with less experience

obesity a condition where a person is very overweight

politics having to do with running for and holding public office

priority something that is more important than other things

stadium a large building where events, such as concerts, are held

veterans people who have served in the military

working-class related to people who do jobs that often require manual labor

Index

Becoming 4, 20, 22
Chicago 4, 6, 10-12
First Lady 4, 16, 22
Harvard 8-9, 22
law 8-10, 22
Let's Move! 16, 22
Obama, Barack 10, 12, 14, 22
Obama, Malia 14
Obama, Sasha 14
obesity 16
Princeton 8
Robinson, Craig 6
school 8-10, 18, 22
veterans 18
White House, The 14, 16-17, 20

Read More

Schwartz, Heather E. *Michelle Obama: Political Icon (Boss Lady Bios)*. Minneapolis: Lerner Publications, 2021.

Stoltman, Joan. *Michelle Obama (Little Biographies of Big People)*. New York: Gareth Stevens, 2018.

Learn More Online

1. Go to **www.factsurfer.com**
2. Enter "**Michelle Obama**" into the search box.
3. Click on the cover of this book to see a list of websites.

About the Author

Rachel Rose is a writer who lives in San Francisco. Her favorite books to write are about people who lead inspiring lives.